Aesop's Fables

KINGFISHER
Published in the United States by Kingfisher, an imprint of Henry Holt and Company
LLC, 175 Fifth Avenue, New York, New York 10010. First published in Great Britain by
Kingfisher Publications plc, an imprint of Macmillan Children's Books, London.

Distributed in Canada by H. B. Fenn and Company Ltd.

Library of Congress Cataloging-in-Publication Data
Aesop's fables/Saviour Pirotta; illustrated by Richard Johnson.
p. cm.
Summary: A collection of eight fables, each introduced by Aesop, the freed slave turned master
storyteller, who shares the real-life events that inspired each tale.
1. Aesop's fables—Adaptions. 2. Fables, Greek—Adaptions. [1. Fables. 2. Folklore.]
I. Johnson, Richard, ill. II. Aesop. III. Title.
PZ8.2.P46Aes 2005
398.2—dc21
[E]
2005027423

ISBN: 978-0-7534-6133-4

Kingfisher books are available for special promotions and premiums.
For details contact: Director of Special Markets, Holtzbrinck Publishers.

Printed in China
2 4 6 8 10 9 7 5 3
2TR/0108/SNPLFG/SGCH(SGCH)/140MA/C

Aesop's Fables

SAVIOUR PIROTTA
ILLUSTRATED BY RICHARD JOHNSON

KINGFISHER
NEW YORK

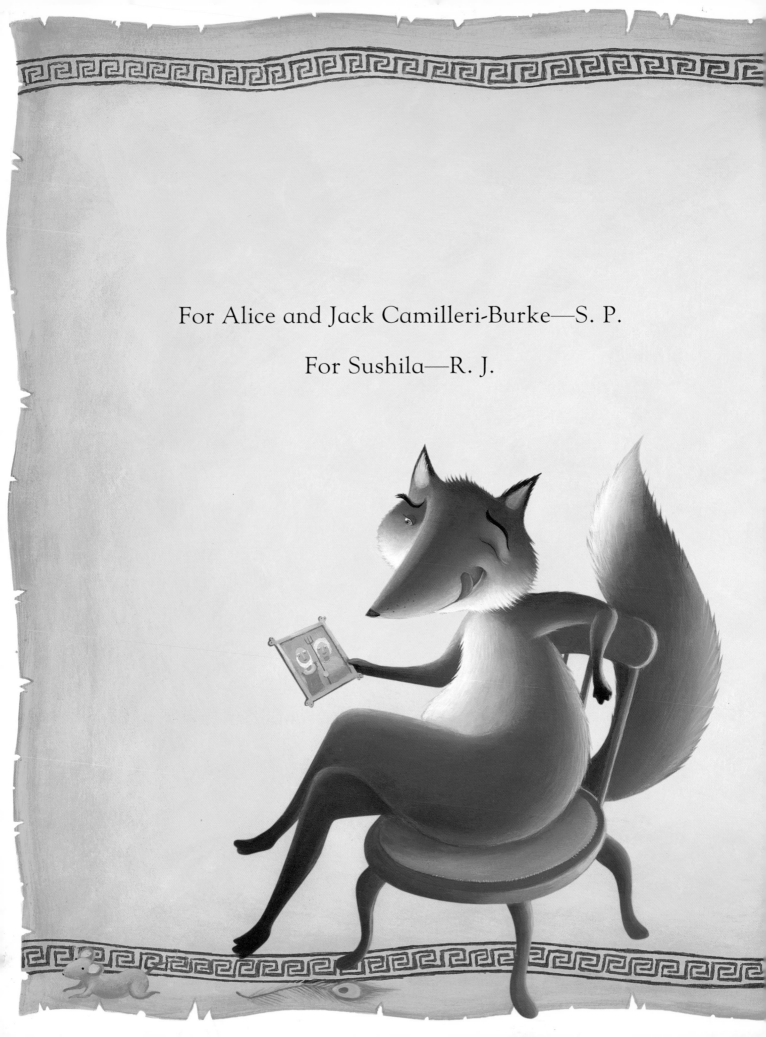

For Alice and Jack Camilleri-Burke—S. P.

For Sushila—R. J.

CONTENTS

THE CAT'S BELL

Welcome, friends and strangers—make yourselves comfortable! If you are looking for entertainment, then you have come to the right place. My name is Aesop—some of you might have heard of me. I am a storyteller. Some say I am the greatest storyteller ever, but I don't know about that.

My fables are short and simple. They are mostly about animals and simple country folk, not brave heroes and their mighty deeds. If you listen carefully, you might notice that each one of them contains a message for my listeners, to teach them how to be happy and wise.

Sometimes people ask me if I remember when I told my first story. The truth is, I do not. Even as a boy, working endlessly in my master's fields, ideas would come into my head, and I would entertain my friends with them. I was born a slave, and slaves do not have anything to call their own except for their voices. But I do remember when I first told one of my favorite stories—I was very young. Along with two of the other young slaves in my master's household, I had been caught nibbling stew and was severely beaten.

My friends—their bottoms stinging with pain—suggested that we should run away. We could steal some of the master's gold, they said, and use it to go to sea. We could join a band of pirates, who grow rich by plundering ships and holding princes for ransom. They did not consider what would happen if we got caught, or if the pirates refused to take us, or even if we got seasick. So, to teach them a lesson about making plans, I told them this story—*The Cat's Bell*.

**I**n the hills around Athens there was a farm, and on that farm lived a great many mice—hundreds and hundreds of mice. As the farmer was old and almost blind, they had free rein of the place. Golden-furred mice nested in the cornfield. Pearly-gray mice set up their homes in the grain supply, nibbling through the sacks with their pointy teeth. There were mice in the dairy, mice in the pantry, mice in the manger—and even mice in the pillows. Oh, those mice! They lived like lords and ladies, until one morning the farmer found mouse droppings in his breakfast honey. Then he upped and bought himself a cat!

What a monstrous creature that cat seemed to the tiny mice. Covered in bristly fur, she spent all day and night hunting her unfortunate victims. She waited for them outside their mouse holes. She stalked them on swift, soundless paws. When she pounced, her teeth and claws were as sharp as the Grim Reaper's blade.

At last the mice could take no more. They had to do something about that monster of a cat; too many of them were disappearing down her ever-hungry throat. But what could they do? How could small, defenseless creatures like them get the best of a hulking brute like her?

The oldest mouse on the farm called a meeting in the orange grove behind the farmhouse, where both field mice and house mice could gather without straying too far from their homes. They met late one afternoon, when the cat was taking a nap on top of the garden wall. Row after row of mice assembled under the trees: brown ones and black ones, gray ones and marmalade-orange ones, all with trembling, delicate whiskers.

Every mouse had something to say—an idea to suggest, an opinion to discuss, a horror story to tell. "That cat crept up on my children while they were nibbling on a piece of rope."

"She pounced on my little ones while they were playing in the kitchen garden."

"So how can we protect ourselves?" interrupted the oldest mouse. "Let's concentrate on that for the moment."

Some of the mice put forward ridiculous proposals:

"Lock the kitty in the barn."

"Push her down a deep hole."

"Or a well!"

"Throw her in the river! Cats are scared of water. She'll soon be squealing as loudly as the rest of us."

"It's not enough to get rid of the cat," said the oldest mouse. "The farmer will simply get another one."

Three white mice put up their paws to speak. Everyone quieted down at once, for although they were young, the white mice were considered very smart. They had recently made their home in the wooden chest where the farmer kept his legal documents and had devoured scrolls of wisdom.

"The trouble with cats," said the first of the white mice, "is that they make absolutely no noise as they creep up on us. Owls rustle their wings, snakes hiss with their tongues, but cats are silent. There's nothing— not a whisper or a hint of a sound."

"The solution to our dilemma is very simple," said the second white mouse. "Any fool can see what needs to be done. All we need is a bell. A little bell and a piece of ribbon."

All the other mice looked at each other, wondering if their ears were playing tricks on them. What could they do with a bell and a piece of ribbon?

The third clever mouse cleared his throat. "If one of us creeps up on the cat and ties the bell around her neck while she's sleeping, we'll all be safe. You see, the bell will jingle every time the monster moves. That way we can all hear her when she tries to creep up on us, and we'll be able to flee before she pounces."

A roar of approval greeted the third mouse's words. What a wonderful idea! And so simple, too. Who would have thought? A little bell and a piece of ribbon! Only the three wise mice could have concocted such an excellent plan.

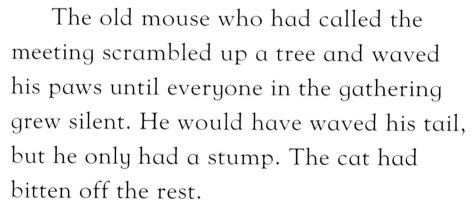

The old mouse who had called the meeting scrambled up a tree and waved his paws until everyone in the gathering grew silent. He would have waved his tail, but he only had a stump. The cat had bitten off the rest.

"The white mice's plan is indeed clever and daring," he said. "But which one of us is going to tie the bell around the cat's neck?"

An immediate silence fell over the gathering. All eyes turned to the garden wall, where the cat was still asleep. Even from a distance, everyone could see the powerful muscles rippling under her fur.

"We're too small to climb up the cat's back," gulped the field mice.

"One of us would do it, but we're too noisy to approach a sleeping cat," squeaked the grain-supply mice. "The monster would wake up before we had time to tie on the bell."

"And we reek of cheese," cried the dairy mice. "The cat would smell a rat . . ."

Up on the garden wall the cat woke up and yawned. She'd been sleeping for quite a while, and her tummy was rumbling with hunger. Her eyes reflected the setting sun as she looked around, seeking prey. What was that she could see under the orange trees? Was it a horde of silly but succulent mice?

The cat chuckled, licked her lips, and with a graceful leap, landed on the ground. She made no noise as she sprinted through the grass. Before the mice noticed she was close, she sprang right into the middle of the gathering, her teeth bared, her claws outstretched. The mice bolted in all directions, squealing and squeaking and shuddering with fear.

And that was the last of their clever plan!

· MORAL ·
It is easy to come up with ideas, but it is harder to put them into action.

THE LION AND THE MOUSE

Welcome back, my friends. Do you want to hear another fable?

People often ask me what it feels like to be a free man after spending so many years of my life as a slave. Words cannot express my joy every time I remember that I can decide for myself what is best for me. I can work for others, not because I have been ordered to, but because I want to help of my own free will.

I had two masters before I gained my freedom, both men who lived on the island of Samos. The first man was named Xanthus, and the second, Jadmon. Jadmon, a merchant by trade, was a strict master, but he also respected wit and learning. I helped him out of many scrapes with my stories; I taught his children too. As a reward, Jadmon gave me my freedom, so I could travel anywhere I wanted, visiting all the wonderful places I had heard about from merchants who had dined with Jadmon.

And I did travel—by boat, by mule, even on foot. Everywhere I went, I learned new things and heard stories that I could adapt for my own use. I talked to everyone I met, making friends with high-ranking officials, but also with cooks and serving maids. Many have frowned on my habit of befriending slaves and servants. But let me tell you, friendship and wisdom can be found anywhere. And friends are not measured by their wealth and status in life, but by their deeds, as you will see in this fable—
The Lion and the Mouse . . .

On the vast plains of Africa lived a honey-colored mouse. She had no less than eight children—all constantly mewling to be fed—so she was always rushed off her little paws looking for food. As soon as the sun set, the mouse would creep out of her hole, and if the coast was clear, she would set off in search of nibbles. She managed to bring home some tasty tidbits too—grains of corn and rice, sunflower seeds blown across the plain by the wind, and sometimes even grapes from the wild vines that grew in the dry soil.

One night the mouse spied a traveler. He was walking along the dirt road, eating as he went. Crumbs fell from his hands as he broke bread and cheese to share with his dog.

"What a feast for my children," said the mouse to herself, and she followed the traveler along the dusty path, picking up the crumbs.

By dawn she had strayed far from home. Suddenly realizing that the sun was about to rise, she panicked and started back. Before long she found herself in front of a mountain all covered in dry, golden-yellow grass that blew around in the breeze. Was it wheat? Corn?

Millet, waiting to ripen? The mouse had a little nibble. Ugh! The strange grass was too tough to eat.

She scampered farther up the mountain, wondering where on earth she was. Then she spied something caught in the billowing grass—a stray grain of corn. The mouse pounced and bit into it, and a mouthful of the strange grass came away between her teeth.

All at once there was an earthquake; the mountain shook violently. The mouse tried to hold onto the golden-yellow grass, but she was thrown off—only to be caught in a vicelike grip that threatened to crush her bones. Razor-sharp claws wrapped themselves around her, pressing into her fur, and a loud roar made her ears ring. Two eyes as wide as full moons glowered at her from above.

The poor mouse had been caught by a lion. The mountain she had wandered into was not part of the landscape at all—it was the lion's mane.

"Who dares to wake me from my sleep?" roared the lion, and his eyes blazed with fury.

"I'm sorry," squeaked the mouse. "I didn't mean to disturb you. I thought your mane was a mountain."

"A mountain, eh?" growled the lion, almost deafening the little mouse. "Are you suggesting that I am as old as the hills?"

You see, the lion was getting on in years, and he was very touchy about it. Only the night before he'd been unable to catch a gazelle he was chasing—a failure he was mightily glad that none of his friends had witnessed.

"I'm not suggesting anything," cried the mouse. "I'm only a small, humble rodent."

"You are small," said the lion. "But you'll do for breakfast."

"Don't eat me, please," begged the mouse. "I have eight children. If I don't return home, they'll starve to death."

"Why should I care about your miserable little brood?"

asked the lion, and he raised the mouse to his lips. His mouth looked like the jaws of death to her, the poor thing.

"Please!" shrieked the mouse, kicking her little paws frantically against the lion's sharp, cheesy-yellow teeth. "Let me go. I'm no more to you than a crumb of bread is to a human."

The lion ignored her cries. Now he could boast to his friends that he had gobbled up another animal in one mouthful—he just had to be careful not to mention that the animal was a harmless little mouse.

"If you let me go," squeaked the mouse, as the lion's teeth grazed her tail, "I will repay your kindness."

"What?" roared the lion. "What use could you possibly be to me?"

"I have no idea," the mouse had to admit. "But my skills might come in handy for you one day. You—you never know."

The lion burst out laughing. "You are the boldest creature I have ever met," he roared. "Imagine thinking that a worthless rodent like you could help the king of the animals." So tickled was he by the ridiculousness of the suggestion that he opened his paw to let the mouse go. His victim disappeared in a flash.

The lion went back to sleep. When he woke up again, the sun was setting behind the distant mountains. The mighty beast yawned. His tummy was rumbling with hunger. How he wished he'd eaten that little mouse after all. Even a crumb is better than nothing to someone who's starving.

As he sat there, regretting his rash decision to let the mouse go, the lion heard something bleating. It was a goat. A farmer had tied her to a tree and left her there. The poor creature had caught the smell of the lion on the wind and was terrified. Without a moment's hesitation, the lion ran through the long grass, his sharp claws at the ready.

But he never got to the goat. As he approached the tree, the ground seemed to open under his feet, and he found himself falling into a steep-sided pit. He landed with a bump on hard, stony earth.

The poor lion had been tricked. The goat was nothing but bait to lure him into a hunters' trap.

The hunters, laughing and shaking their spears, peered over the edge of the pit.

"You'll make a fine pet for our king," they jeered, "and when you die, your fur will be turned into a cozy rug for his royal feet."

They started pulling on ropes, which they'd hidden under a blanket of dead leaves, and the poor lion realized that the pit was lined with a net. The hunters drew it so tightly around him that he couldn't open his mouth wide enough to snap. Slowly, like sailors hoisting the mainsail, the hunters dragged him out of the pit. They tied him, still trapped in the net, to a stout pole that they carried on their shoulders. Then off they went, singing as they walked:

The eagle soars,
The tiger roars,
The king of the beasts is fallen.

The panther prowls,
The hyena howls,
The king of the beasts is fallen.

"What a fool I've been," thought the lion to himself, swinging from the pole like a bunch of grapes. "Why, oh why did I not look before I leaped?"

Toward morning the hunters stopped for a rest. The lion was a heavy beast, and they were exhausted. One of the hunters lit a fire, and after eating some bread and meat the men fell asleep.

The lion tried to go to sleep too, but he couldn't. His mane was itching terribly. Something was scurrying around in his fur. The lion desperately wanted to scratch it, but he was unable to move a single claw.

"It must be fleas," he thought sadly. "What a sorry end for the king of the beasts."

But the creatures scurrying around in the lion's mane were not fleas. They were somewhat bigger, and they moved

around with amazing speed.

"What's going on?" wondered the lion. Then he heard a familiar voice.

"Remember me?"

It was the little mouse that he'd freed the day before.

"I heard the hunters' song as they came past my hole," said the mouse, climbing out of the lion's mane and onto his nose. "And when I realized it was you they were singing about, I brought my children out to meet you."

"Are they running all over my mane?" asked the lion through clenched teeth. "They're as impertinent as fleas."

"My children are always hungry," said the mouse. "They nibble everything they find."

Suddenly the net fell from around the lion's head, freeing his mouth. A few moments later, his front paws were free too. The lion shook himself, and the rest of the bindings came apart. Little mice, strands of rope stuck between their teeth, tumbled out of his mane.

"See?" laughed the mouse. "They even nibble on rope. I keep telling them it's not good for them, but they never listen."

The lion stood up on his four legs, free at last.

"Thank you, little mouse," he purred. "You saved me from a fate worse than death."

"It's my pleasure," said the mouse. "After all, you spared my life." Her children gathered around her, their eyes catching the light of the rising sun.

"Goodbye, little mice," roared the lion, and he leaped away into the tall grass. His roar woke up the hunters, who picked up their spears and began chasing him, leaving the rest of the food behind them. The mouse and her children had a wonderful feast of bread and meat, I can tell you. They'd never eaten so much in all their lives.

And the mighty lion? The hunters didn't catch him. Legend has it that he never hurt another small creature again—not even a flea.

· M O R A L ·
Little friends make
great friends.

The Wolf and the Dog

It's time for another story, my friends! And once again, it comes from my experiences in life.

Many people have asked me if I was happy when I was a slave. My answer is always the same. I always yearned to be free, even though my master was kind and did not beat me or send me to bed hungry. Some people said that I was lucky to be a slave, sure of having enough food every day and a warm bed to sleep in at night. Many poor people, they pointed out, were much worse off than I was, even if they could claim to be free. They lived in squalor, went to bed hungry, and if they ever got sick, no doctor was fetched to cure them.

I was aware of all this, but I couldn't help thinking of a wolf I'd once seen up in the hills. He looked mangy, and his ribs showed through his fur. There were fleas in his coat too; I could see them jumping around. Yet he looked me straight in the eye as I went past. I never forgot that look—the look of a free spirit.

That same day I saw a fat dog trotting along with his master. His coat was shiny, the sign of a well-fed animal. He was clean—he had probably been scrubbed and perfumed by the master's slaves that very morning. Yet there was something sad about him as he watched some stray dogs running free around him. His eyes were full of longing. That evening I made up this story about *The Wolf and the Dog*.

he wild places of Greece are full of wolves. They are always hungry, always on the move, traveling in packs, in search of prey among the boulders and stunted trees of the outlands.

One such wolf was born high up in the mountains of Crete. His mother fed him and took care of him until he was able to fend for himself. Then she let him go out into the wild, so that he could take his rightful place with the pack that hunted on the mountain. It was spring when the wolf cub left his mother's lair, which he'd shared with six brothers and sisters. The older wolves welcomed him with fierce baying that rang through the mountain. He quickly learned to hunt, to search for food with his nose, to stalk deer and goats, and to steal lambs from the snoozing shepherds and their huge,

fluffy-coated dogs. When the hunt was successful, there was always a great feast, and the whole pack joined in. Then the mountains echoed with wolf songs from dusk till dawn.

But the spring turned into summer and summer into winter, and with the winter came freezing winds and snow that settled on the wolf's once glossy coat, turning it into a heavy burden of ice. There were no more goats to be stalked, nor deer, nor wild boar. The shepherds moved their flocks down into the valley for shelter. The smaller creatures that the pack had ignored in the warmer months now burrowed deep into the earth to sleep. Soon the earth froze under the wolf's paws so that he could barely run without slipping. One by one the elders of the pack died, and those that survived grew thin with hunger. The wolves' coats turned mangy and coarse.

On the rare occasions when a little food was to be had, there was no feasting, no celebration. The wolves quarreled among themselves, the strong pushing the weak away in a selfish bid to get more meat. The young wolf started hiding in a cave, where he would sit for hours on end, wondering if the spring, the sun, and the good times would ever return.

Then late one evening he heard human voices carried by the wind. There were sounds of horses neighing, bells ringing, and musical instruments being played. The wolf peeped out of the cave and saw a band of pilgrims returning home after offering sacrifices to the old mountain gods. Some—the rich ones—rode horses and wore expensive furs wrapped around their shoulders. Servants in plainer clothes rode along behind them on donkeys. There were children on foot, too, each one carrying a heavy basket or a chest strapped to their backs. Dogs—not the huge, fluffy kind that watched over the lambs in the summer, but smaller ones with dark coats—wove their way through people's legs, barking and yelping. Bringing up the rear were the slaves, their carts laden with enormous pots and cages of fat chickens.

The sight of those chickens drew the wolf toward the band of pilgrims as helplessly as a twig is drawn by a river's current. He slunk out of the cave and followed them, saliva dribbling from his mouth. But he didn't get too close. He knew that a lone wolf had to find the right time to pounce— perhaps at night, if the moon slipped behind thick clouds, or early in the morning, when the mist wrapped itself like a shroud around the mountain.

The next minute an older man with a walking stick announced, "We'll rest here for the night," and the travelers stopped. People got off their horses, the older ones helped  by their servants. Grooms unsaddled the donkeys and led them to a stream where they could drink. A group of women lit a fire, placed pots upon it, and brought food out of the hampers to cook over the flames. The smell of cooking filled the air, and the young wolf could not help himself. He edged closer and closer to the camp, his tummy rumbling with acute hunger.

Eventually someone spotted him. "Look out, a wolf!" People leaped to their feet in alarm. The old man with the walking stick started trembling uncontrollably. A cook screamed, and the servants reached for axes and clubs. The wolf, knowing that he was weak from cold and lack of food, quickly melted back into the shadows.

"Not much of a life, is it—skulking in the darkness, trembling at the sight of clubs and axes?" It was one of the dark-coated dogs speaking. He was returning from the nearby stream.

"Times are hard, brother. You do everything you can to survive," the wolf said grimly.

The dog sat on a rock, looking around him with disdain. "Just look at this place," he said. "Bare rocks, the wind howling around your ears all the time, and nothing to keep out the cold. I don't know how you survive. In my master's house we sleep in baskets lined with velvet, right next to a warm fire. And we never go hungry. Meals come piping hot, in pretty dishes. Why don't you come with us and live in a palace?"

"I admit, it does sound tempting," said the wolf. "But I am not a dog. I would get thrown out."

"You could pass for a dog," said his friend. "There are many of us in my master's house. Trust me, you will be safe."

The wolf imagined himself eating hot meals out of fancy dishes, snoozing contentedly by the fire, and playing with his new friends without a care in the world.

"I'll come," he said.

Early the next morning he set off with the pilgrims, walking close to his new friend. As the sun came up, he couldn't help noticing how glossy the dog's coat was and how brightly his eyes shone in the morning light. At the foot of the mountain they came to a

plain, and in the distance they could see the walls of a city.

"Your new home," said the dog.

The wolf turned to bid the mountain farewell.

"Come on," said the dog. "You'll get left behind." He leaned forward to nudge the wolf on.

"What's that strange mark around your neck?" the wolf asked. "It seems as if the fur has been worn away."

"It's nothing," said the dog. "In my master's house all dogs are marked like this. It's where the leather collar chafes our necks."

"A collar?"

"The master ties us up sometimes, when he doesn't want us to roam around, or when he wants to take us to a particular place."

The wolf looked puzzled. "You mean, you let someone chain you up?"

"You get used to it after a while," said the dog.

The wolf turned and looked at the mountain again. "The wild is a harsh place," he said. "But there are no chains there, no collars, no one to stop me from roaming around of my own free will."

"Think of the comfort," the dog urged him. "All that good food. Isn't it worth a collar around your neck?"

The wolf shook his head. "I'd rather starve as a free animal than feast in chains. Good-bye, my friend."

And with that he turned and bounded back up the mountain toward his cave, his nights of hunger, his old hunting grounds, his cherished freedom.

· MORAL ·
Freedom is
priceless.

THE GOOSE THAT LAID THE GOLDEN EGGS

Greetings once more, my listeners. It is time for another of my little fables.

I once told a story to King Croesus of Lydia, whose empire is so close to my beloved Greece. He enjoyed it so much that he asked me to stay on in Sardis, his dazzling capital city. That way he could call on me whenever he wanted to listen to a fable. I met many famous people at his court, including philosophers, engineers, and famous lawmakers visiting from Greece.

One morning I came across the king in his garden, sitting at a table. He seemed angry, and as I approached, he knocked a cup of wine to the ground. "It is said that the Persian palace of Cyrus the Great makes mine look like a henhouse," he thundered. "Well, I am going to raze this chicken coop to the ground and build one even greater than my enemy's."

"I hesitate to argue with a noble king," I said meekly, "but where is the money for such a building to come from?"

"We have gold in the mines," snapped King Croesus. "And there is more in the sands of the River Pactolus. I shall order my slaves to find every last shining nugget of it. And if I run out of money, I shall tax the people."

"'Tax the people,'" I echoed sadly. "The people find life hard enough as it is, without paying more taxes for a king's foible. The people love you, sire, but I would hesitate to try and get more money out of their already empty pockets. Listen to the story about *The Goose That Laid the Golden Eggs.*"

A farmer and his wife lived high up in the mountains. They were poor, penniless folk, but they had a lot to be thankful for, just the same. Their home was a pretty cottage right beside a brook, from which they drew fresh, clean water. They had chickens in the yard and a goat to give them milk. In the summer their olive trees were laden with fruits— most of which they turned into oil.

"We don't need for anything up here," the farmer's wife used to tell passing hunters, who came up the mountains in search of deer.

One day the farmer went to the market on his donkey, making his way carefully down the mountain trail. On his way back he met an old woman who was picking herbs in the evening mist.

"Good evening," said the old woman to the farmer, casting a beady eye on the wicker baskets strapped to the donkey's flanks. "What nice things have you bought for the lucky missus?"

"I couldn't afford much," admitted the farmer, "but I bought a length of homespun cloth so that my wife can make a new apron. I purchased some good wine and salted fish, too. It's a treat for us because we don't often eat fish up here in the mountains."

"Indeed, I haven't tasted fish for years," agreed the old lady.

"Why don't you have some of mine?" said the farmer. "I've bought plenty." And he took a sharp-smelling package from his basket and thrust it into her gnarled hands.

"I would like to repay your kindness," said the old lady. And she clapped her wizened hands and called out in a strange tongue that the farmer could not understand. Suddenly she was surrounded by geese that came, flapping their feathery wings, out of the mist.

"Here," chuckled the old woman, scooping up one of the geese. "Take this one. It'll give you nice eggs."

The man put the goose in the basket, buckling down the lid so that it wouldn't escape. When he got home, he let the goose free in the yard, where it started jostling with the hens for grubs.

The next morning when the farmer's wife went out to the hens, she discovered that the goose had laid an egg—an enormous one. She picked it up.

"Pah," she said, surprised at how heavy it was. "My eyes deceived me; it's just a stone." She was about to throw it away when the sun came out from behind a cloud and shone on the egg, making it glitter.

Puzzled, the farmer's wife wiped it clean on a corner of her new apron. The egg seemed to be made out of gold—but how could that be?

"Who gave you this goose?" she asked her husband.

"An old woman," replied the farmer. "I met her picking herbs at dusk."

"She must have been a kind witch," said his wife. "I think her goose has laid a golden egg."

The farmer couldn't believe his eyes. He saddled the donkey again and went to see a gold merchant at the market. Yes, the egg really was made of gold, pure gold. He got a hefty sum for it, enough to buy some fine cloth for his wife, some tools for himself, and a big flagon of wine. He bought some fish, too—not the cheap salted sardines he'd purchased the previous day, but expensive fresh ones, caught in the sea the night before.

The next morning the goose laid another golden egg. And she kept on laying one egg after another until the farmer

had filled a basket with them. Soon the farmer and his wife had become quite wealthy. They wore fine clothes and rode to the market on horses. They ate fresh food out of expensive bowls. In the summer they repaired and repainted the cottage and built a dairy next to it, where they kept a herd of cows.

You would have thought that all this unexpected luck would have made the farmer happy. But not so! Every morning as he polished a new golden egg, he fretted and worried.

"What if someone steals the magic goose?" he'd tell his wife. "What would we do if the creature got sick and died? We wouldn't grow any richer. In fact, we'd soon be poor again."

"Stop fretting, love. No one is going to steal the goose," his wife assured him. "Only the hunters ever make it this far up the mountain, and they never come anywhere near the farm. As for the goose herself, she won't live forever, of course, so I have put some money aside in case of emergencies. We have enough dried food to last us all year, too. And when that's all used up, we have the cows for milk, the chickens for eggs, and the field for growing crops. We have more than enough to see us comfortably through our old age."

But the farmer couldn't stop worrying. All that good luck was spoiled by his constant fretting. Then one morning a terrible and foolish thought hatched in his mind.

"I must lay my hands on all the golden eggs now," he said to himself. "All at once, before it's too late."

That very same day, while his wife was visiting a friend farther down the mountain, he grabbed the goose and twisted her neck expertly with his bare hands. He did it so quickly and gently that the goose hardly felt a thing. Then he cut the dead bird open with a knife. Imagine his horror when he found no hoard of golden eggs inside it—only a single soft yolk without a golden shell.

And that was not all. There was more misfortune to come. As the tiny yolk curdled in the farmer's hand, all the wealth that had come with the goose disappeared into thin air. The tools, the bowls, the fine clothes, the wine, the horses—even the cows and the dairy—vanished.

"Oh husband, what on earth have you done?" said the farmer's wife when she returned home to find her house shabby and rickety once more.

Her husband was so racked with grief that he couldn't answer. The poor woman tried to console him, but not a word she said could make him feel better. Sobbing like a child, he saddled the donkey and rode out to find the witch who had given him the golden goose. Perhaps she would give him another, and this time he would not let greed get the better of him. But he never met the wise woman again. People say he wanders around the mountain looking for her to this very day, while his wife sits at home, sighing for the days when they were happy with the little that they had.

· MORAL ·
Be content with
your good fortune.

The Fox and the Stork

Welcome back, my listeners. Once again it is time for me to tell another story.

I sometimes traveled with King Croesus himself, to visit many of the kingdoms that make up my beloved Greece. It was the perfect opportunity to see how people lived—from the mighty kings on their thrones to the poorest workmen and slaves in their masters' workshops.

I remember one king did not treat Croesus with the respect that he deserved. The food was tasteless and mediocre. The beds in the guest chambers were lumpy, and I shall not even mention the awfulness of the wine. Croesus was so annoyed that he threatened to leave the palace. Indeed, he threatened to have it pulled down stone by stone. But we were there to sign an important treaty, so I begged Croesus to keep his peace.

On the way back home he fumed. "I shall get my revenge on that tightfisted king. Oh, the shame of being humiliated in front of other kings."

"The shame is on the tightfisted king, your majesty," I said. "He shall go down in history as an ignorant fool whose manners outraged the great Croesus."

"I shall invite him to my palace next year," Croesus spat. "Then let us see how he likes eating stale fish."

"It is not worth the trouble, my lord," I ventured. "Once a fool, always a fool. Besides, where will this desire for petty revenge lead? I will tell you one of my fables as we travel. It is called *The Fox and the Stork*."

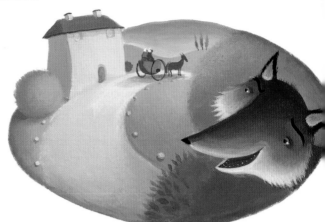

In the farmland outside Delphi lived a young fox. He was the farmers' biggest enemy, for he preyed on their ducks and broke into their henhouses.

Early one morning the fox heard a cart trundling along the road. He peeped through the undergrowth and spied a farmer and his wife on their way to the market. Knowing that their house would be empty, the fox hurried there, only to find that the farmer had penned the geese in with the hens, and his wife had locked the henhouse door. The fox was leaving when he noticed that an upstairs window was slightly ajar. Quick as a flash, he scampered up a nearby vine and squeezed in through the open window. A delicious smell filled his nostrils, and he hurried down to the kitchen.

What a feast met his eyes! Fresh sausages hung from big hooks in the ceiling. Ripe cheeses, each one as big as the wheel of a cart, were piled in a corner. There were jars of olives and bottles of wine and baskets of gleaming nuts just waiting to be shelled. The fox had hardly started to dig in when he heard someone coming down the path. Was it the farmer's friend or a neighbor who was keeping an eye on the place? The fox had no intention of finding out. He grabbed all he could carry—sausages and cheese and olives—and made a hasty retreat out of the upstairs window.

Back home on the edge of the farmland he began cooking a delicious meal. He stoked the fire and boiled the water. He chopped up the meat and the cheese and popped them in the pot with the olives. Soon a delicious smell filled his home. The fox sat on his doorstep, enjoying the breeze while waiting for the food to cook.

"What a delicious smell," said the deer, who lived next door to the fox. She'd just come out of her house with the stork, a big bird who had a home in the reeds nearby.

"It's making my tummy rumble with hunger," exclaimed the stork. "Is it your cooking we can smell, Fox?"

"It is," said the fox proudly.

"I never smelled anything so scrumptious in all my life," said the deer.

"Why don't you come in and have some?" said the fox. "It'll be ready soon."

"I can't stay," said the deer, who had been invited to lunch somewhere else. "But perhaps Stork will."

The stork smiled timidly. "If I'm not imposing . . . "

The fox didn't really want to share his lunch with the stork. He'd only invited the deer because he owed her a favor. But now he was trapped, because if he turned the stork away, the deer was sure to think that he was mean and ungracious.

"It would be a pleasure to have you," said the fox to the stork. "Please, come in."

The stork helped the fox set the table. By now the smell of the stew was making her mouth water. The fox ladled it out onto big, flat plates, humming with pleasure when he saw how the sausages had burst their skins and the cheese had gone nicely soft and gooey.

What a feast the fox had. His big tongue lapped up every morsel of that stew. But the poor stork hardly ate a thing. However hard she tried, she could only dip the tip of her beak in the food, and her tongue could not reach any of that delicious meat.

The cruel fox had chosen the shallow plates on purpose. He knew that the stork could not eat off them.

"I see you haven't touched your food," he smirked as he licked his plate clean. "Perhaps it was not good enough."

"On the contrary," said the stork, trying to hide her disappointment. "It was quite a feast. You must come to my house tomorrow. I'll repay you with a fine dinner of my own."

"I'd be delighted," said the fox, who'd heard that the stork was an accomplished cook herself.

So the next day at sunset the fox knocked on the stork's door. The aroma of fish and sweet onions was wafting out of the windows. The fox had eaten nothing all day with the intention of stuffing himself at the stork's expense. He could feel his mouth starting to water uncontrollably.

"Good evening," he called.

The stork welcomed him into her home with open wings. "Dinner's ready," she said. "I hope you're hungry." And she showed the fox to the table, where two places had been set.

"What are we having?" asked the fox. "Is it a pie, a stew, or a soup?"

"It's a surprise," said the stork. "Close your eyes, and I'll bring it in."

The fox did as he was asked. He heard the stork going to the kitchen and returning; he heard her put something on the table, something that smelled so delicious that he almost fainted at the thought of wolfing it down.

"You can open your eyes now."

The fox did so immediately, his tongue ready to start lapping up the food. But what do you know—the stork had made a stew, but she'd served it in tall, narrow beakers!

"Dig in before it gets cold," she said, pretending not to notice the angry look in the fox's eyes. "I've made lots. Enough for second helpings."

Poor Fox. He tried to stick his snout down the beaker, he tried to reach past the narrow neck with his tongue, he even tried to suck the food up. No matter what he did, that delicious food remained firmly out of reach. He thought about smashing the beaker on the floor, but he knew that the din would attract the neighbors' attention, and he'd be the laughingstock of the farmlands.

"Thank you for a wonderful meal," he said to the stork. And holding his head up high, he returned home even hungrier than he'd been when he left. Needless to say, he never played a horrible trick on the stork again—or on anyone else, for that matter.

· MORAL ·
Treat others as you'd like them to treat you.

THE TORTOISE AND THE HARE

Ah, thank you for coming to hear another story, my dear friends. Storytellers, as well as poets and playwrights, are always asked where they get their ideas. From real life, I always answer. Look around you, watch what people are doing, listen to their arguments and conversations, and you will find a lot of inspiration and ideas for stories.

Take today, for example. After breakfast I went for a walk in the vineyards, to admire this year's harvest. In a field I came across two young brothers who were both weeding a vegetable patch. One of the men was working slowly, carefully uprooting all the weeds that might choke his crops one day. The other, however, worked hastily, missing a lot of weeds and trampling on his precious seedlings.

"Why are you in such a hurry to finish?" I asked.

"My father always praises my brother for his work,"

he replied. "I am going to finish first today. My father will be pleased with me for a change, not him."

"Forgive me for saying this," I said, "but you are leaving a lot of weeds behind. Your father will send you back to do the work all over again when he sees what you have done. Is it not better to do the work slowly but correctly, like your brother, than to rush and fail your task?"

The young man didn't understand what I meant, so I thought of a story. The sun was getting hot, so the brothers and I sat in the shade of a tree to share some figs. While we ate, I told them about *The Tortoise and the Hare.*

Once there was a young hare who could run incredibly fast. If the animals had their own Olympic games, he would undoubtedly have won medals and a garland for his running. Now one day the hare came across some animals at the edge of a field. They had stopped to drink at a pond. They were all talking about the things that they could do well.

"I can hold my breath underwater," said a duck.

"I can fly a long way without stopping," claimed a swallow.

"I can caw very loudly," stated a crow.

"I can see in the dark," boasted a fox.

"I can run very fast," the hare joined in. "Faster than anyone here." He was carried away by his own bragging. He looked around the pond, grinning foolishly at all the animals.

"I challenge any one of you to a race."

For a moment no one spoke, then a reedy voice piped up from among the cattails.

"I accept the young hare's challenge."

All the animals turned to see an old tortoise, who had been drinking quietly at the edge of the pond. The skin on her face and feet was all wrinkled with age, and her shell was covered in tiny cracks.

"Are you sure?" asked the fox.

"He challenged anyone at the pond, didn't he?" said the tortoise. "That includes me. I accept the challenge."

"So be it," said the hare, trying very hard not to smirk. Imagine an old tortoise with aging, puffed-up legs thinking she could win a race against him! She was crazy!

The fox pointed to an olive tree in the distance, standing alone on top of a steep hill. "The first animal to get to that tree will be the winner," he declared.

The duck marked a starting line on the ground with her bill, while the crow and the swallow flew toward the olive tree, so that they could see who got there first. The hare pranced

around, flexing his four legs, and warming himself up for the race, while the tortoise continued to drink. Running was thirsty work! Then the fox called the competitors to the starting line.

"May the best animal win," called the duck to both the hare and the tortoise.

The fox shouted "go," and the hare leaped off the starting line immediately. He tore across the newly harvested field with the speed of a hunter's arrow, leaving a cloud of summer dust in his wake. The tortoise, on the other hand, took her time to get going. She patiently blew the dust out of her nose and started trundling along the field, dragging her heavy shell behind her.

"She doesn't stand a chance of winning, the poor thing," whispered the duck.

"She'll never even make it to the finish line," agreed the fox.

"We must be kind to her when she loses," said the duck. "I think it was very brave of her to accept the hare's challenge."

Meanwhile the hare had crossed the field and was speeding across a vineyard. The harvest had just been gathered so it was deserted, but there were lots of fallen grapes slowly turning into raisins on the ground. The hare peered ahead. Beyond the vineyard was a vast meadow, and beyond the meadow was the steep hill where the olive tree stood, marking

the finish line. He ran on, his four legs moving surely and swiftly, and before long he reached the meadow, where the sun was very bright.

Behind him the poor tortoise plodded along wearily, her shell a tiring weight on her back. She was only halfway across the field, but she was already wheezing like an old mill wheel. Her eyes were stinging in the heat; her jaw hung open. It was amazing that she didn't collapse.

"That old tortoise can't possibly catch up with me," said the hare to himself. "I might as well have a little rest." And he flopped down in the shade of a bush, panting heavily. All around him were fat buttercups and dandelions nodding their heads in the faint breeze. The hare picked a leaf and nibbled on it. Mmm, its sour juice was like nectar in his parched throat. He lay on his back to enjoy it.

Before he knew it the warm afternoon had lulled the hare into a deep sleep. He dreamed of running from one end of the country to the other, crossing fields and deserts and wonderful cities with straight, wide roads. In every place he stopped to rest people and animals gathered to cheer, to give him cool water, and to shower him with gifts. Kings presented him with bunches of sun-sweetened carrots . . .

When he woke up—the roar of the crowd still ringing in his ears—the sun was setting behind the hill that lay ahead. The hare popped his head over the dandelions, and what did he see? The tortoise was dangerously close to the finish line. She'd plodded right past him, wheezing and coughing loudly, without waking him up.

In a blind panic he leaped to his feet and charged across the meadow. Faster and faster he went, his paws digging up the soil, his whiskers trembling, his eyes fixed on the olive tree that marked the finish line. Very soon he started huffing and puffing. Sweat stung his eyes, but, like the champion he was, he brushed it away and kept running. He couldn't stop, of course. His wizened rival was almost at the finish line.

As the hare reached the crest of the hill, he saw the tortoise slowly lift one sore leg and place it against the tree.

"We declare the tortoise the winner of this race," the swallow and the crow called out, and a host of sparrows flew out of the tree, chirping their congratulations.

The hare was hopping furious. He'd been beaten by an old tortoise. Oh, the ridicule! The shame! Animals would be laughing at his defeat all around the countryside. He hopped away before anyone could talk to him and hid in an old burrow behind a prickly bush. No one would find him there.

The tortoise was declared a hero! If she had been competing in the Olympics, her friends would have made her a crown with leaves from the olive tree. But they gave the tortoise a bunch of crunchy lettuce leaves instead, and she enjoyed them very much.

·MORAL·
Slow and steady
wins the race.

THE FROGS THAT WANTED A KING

Sit back, my gentle listeners, and relax. It's story time again.

King Croesus once sent me to Athens, where the rich people wanted to get rid of their ruler, Pesistratus. "Make them see reason," Croesus begged me.

The task turned out to be harder than I thought. The people of Athens seemed determined to change their ruler. I pointed out that Pesistratus had done a lot for the poor people of Athens. He had reduced taxes. He had helped the sick and the elderly. He had even constructed special water pipes to bring fresh water into the city. "Who else would build such magnificent buildings for his people?" I asked.

"No one," they admitted. "But Pesistratus is a general— a gruff, rough soldier. We want someone more refined."

"But the next ruler might turn out to be selfish and heartless," I warned them. "Don't you understand?

If something is not broken, why try to fix it?"

They looked confused, so in order to convince them,
I told them one of my little stories. It was called *The Frogs That
Wanted a King* . . .

great number of frogs once lived close to Mount Olympus. The water in their pond was deep and lush with weeds, where the mother frogs laid their spawn. The air around the pond teemed with insects that they trapped on their sticky tongues. Best of all, a screen of thick reeds grew up around the water, shielding the frogs from dangerous creatures. Life was one big festival for them, which they celebrated with nonstop swimming and long bouts of croaking at sunrise and sunset.

One day two swallows settled on the reeds to drink. "I am taking a message to the king of the swallows," one of the birds said proudly to the other.

Two young frogs overheard. "You have a king?" they asked.

"All creatures have a king," said the swallow.

"We don't," the young frogs said worriedly.

"You must," insisted the swallow. "He probably lives in another pond. Haven't you ever received messages from him or sent him tributes?"

The frogs hadn't. It dawned on them that they had no ruler, no one to care for them. Suddenly their pond didn't seem like such a paradise after all. Life felt empty and hollow.

As discontent settled on the pond, the eldest and fattest of the frogs called a meeting. "We must ask Zeus, the ruler of all the gods, to send us a king," he said. "Let us pray."

And all the frogs joined hands, closed their eyes, and started croaking in unison:

Oh mighty Zeus,
Whose name we all sing,
Have pity, we beg you,
And send us a king!

Before they'd even finished their prayer, there was a flash of lightning that made them jump, and something huge fell out of the sky. It hit the pond with an earsplitting crash, sending a tidal wave of water onto the grass. The frogs were frightened out of their minds and leaped into the nearby reeds to hide. Then one by one, they all peeped out. There, floating

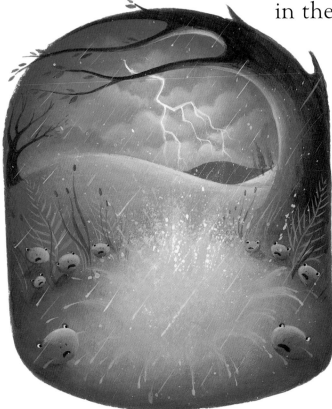

in the pond, lay a hulking monster. It was long, with rough skin, and as silent as the grave.

"It must be our king," whispered the frogs in awe. "Zeus must have answered our prayers."

They summoned up their courage, and making as little noise as possible, they approached their new ruler, who seemed to be asleep. The young frogs made garlands out of water lilies, which they draped all over him.

Even then the king remained silent. The frogs wished that he would talk, if only to give them an order, but he didn't. Still, they were happy to have a ruler, since it made them equal to all the creatures in the world, and they croaked in his honor every sunrise and sunset.

But a week or two later one of the swallows stopped to drink from the pond again. She had delivered her message to the king of the swallows and was on her way back home.

"That's no king," she said, when the frogs showed her the hulking monster in the water. "That's a log, a lump of wood. It must have fallen off a tree."

The frogs were dismayed beyond belief. How could Zeus play such a horrible trick on them? How could he send them a dead piece of wood to be their king?

"We want a real king, a live one," they all said. "One that can speak and give us orders—a ruler as magnificent and impressive as other creatures' kings."

The eldest frog called another meeting in the reeds.

Once again the frogs joined hands, closed their eyes, and started croaking:

> *Oh mighty Zeus,*
> *Whose name we all sing,*
> *Have pity, we beg you,*
> *And send us a REAL king!*

As before there was a flash of lightning that sent the frogs croaking into the reeds. From there they looked up to see a white speck in the sky. Slowly it floated down toward land, like a piece of parchment blown by the winds off Mount Olympus itself. As it got closer, the frogs realized that it was a magnificent bird, the likes of which they had never seen before. He had elegant, long legs and an equally elegant, long neck. Purple feathers adorned his breast.

The bird folded his wings gracefully and came to rest in the water.

"All hail the new king of the frogs. All hail the ruler of the pond." The elder frogs ventured cautiously out from among the reeds, bowing their heads. Their new ruler did not return their greetings. Instead he looked around with his hard, beady eyes and shook his beak, which was long and yellow and had a very sharp tip.

He lifted his wings a little, and as quick as a bolt of lightning from Zeus, he lunged forward. The eldest of the frogs disappeared down his gullet. The others, croaking with terror, dived for cover among the reeds. Zeus, angered that they had not liked their first king, had sent them a heron—a bird whose favorite foods are frogs and fish.

Life was never the same again for those poor, foolish frogs. They lived in constant fear for their lives, only venturing out from their hiding places when their king was away or asleep. And they could never again gather to croak at sunrise and sunset. How they all wished they had never asked Zeus for a ruler. They had been much, much better off without one!

· MORAL ·
Be content with
your lot.

THE JAY AND THE PEACOCKS

Welcome back, dear listeners. This is our last chance to talk together. I must continue on my journey tomorrow. My duties for King Croesus have set me on a course to Delphi. I have enjoyed telling you my tales—indeed, I am sure that I have had as much pleasure from telling them as you have had from listening to them.

I am lucky, for my gift of storytelling has earned me my freedom and a good life. Some of you might like to be storytellers too. You should know that many storytellers do not become rich or famous. I believe that the best ones remain poor and unknown. They tell fables to teach and entertain, not to make money.

Do not be jealous of the rich and mighty, my friends. Don't wish to be powerful, but try to be kind and generous. Do not envy kings, merchants, and princes for their fine clothes and houses. Be content with yourself, your family, and your abilities, for only these things will make you truly happy.

I have one last story to tell you, one that I have told to myself over and over again. It is called *The Jay and the Peacocks*.

n the branches of an ancient oak tree there was a nest made from twigs and leaves, held together with straw and wool. In it lived a mother and father jay and their four children, who cheeped and chirped happily all day long. When the little jays were big enough to fly, their mama and papa showed them how to catch their own worms and how to imitate other birds for fun.

When the biggest jay was seven weeks old and almost a grown-up, he flew over a tall bush and found himself in a king's garden. It was late spring, and the roses were already in bloom. There was a fountain in the middle of the garden, with a host of magnificent peacocks lazing on the grass around it.

The young jay had never seen such dazzling creatures before. The peacocks paraded in front of the fountain, their glossy tails fanned out to catch the light of the sun. Their feathers sparkled and shimmered, a sea of blue and green flecked with gold and jet-black. Suddenly the jay felt embarrassed about his own humble plumage, like a man in a nightmare, who blunders into a temple wearing his everyday rags. He hid in a fig tree.

A servant came out of the palace with a wicker basket and scattered food for the peacocks. A young prince ran out to play among the birds, laughing and admiring their colors. After they had eaten the peacocks all fell asleep, and the jay was able to flutter out of the tree unnoticed. Back home, his mother asked if he'd had a good day.

"It was fine," he said, without his usual enthusiasm, and all that night he could not stop thinking about those peacocks and their gorgeous feathers. In the morning he flew to a pond and, inspecting his sad reflection in the water, sighed, "Oh, how I wish I was a peacock too. Then I could live by the water in the king's garden and be admired by the prince. It would be much more fun than hunting for acorns or looking for worms."

From then on he began hiding in the fig tree every day, watching and envying the peacocks in the garden.

"Come away," said his brothers and sisters when they discovered his secret. "There are lambs in the field, and we have learned to bleat like them. It's much more fun than hiding in this tree."

"Come away from that garden," said his mother, when the young jays told her all about it. "The countryside is teeming with insects for us to catch and eat."

"Come away from that tree," said the jay's father, when the jay's mother had told him why he did not spend time with his family anymore. "I'll show you how to dig holes in the earth so that you may know where to hide acorns when they ripen."

But nothing could lure the young jay away from the king's garden. Spring turned into summer, and the peacocks started to molt, dropping feathers on the grass. The jay had an idea. "Here's my chance to become a peacock," he said to himself. And while the peacocks were asleep in the shade of a rose-covered pergola, he hopped down from his perch and collected the fallen feathers. Before long he had enough to carry out his plan. He found a piece of straw blowing in a bush, and using his claws and beak, he tied the peacock feathers to his own tail.

"Now I am a peacock too," he said happily. And he flew proudly onto the newly cut grass.

"Hello there."

One by one the peacocks lifted their heads and blinked their jewel-like eyes. "Oh look, brothers, there's a new peacock in the garden," said one. "Are you a new gift for the prince? Who sent you? The ruler of wondrous Babylon? The pharaoh of mysterious Egypt?"

They all crowded around to welcome him, creating a terrible din. Then something unexpected and disastrous happened. With all the hugging and pushing and shoving, the straw that bound the peacock feathers to the jay's tail came loose. The feathers fell off.

"What treachery is this?" shrieked one of the peacocks. "You are not a peacock at all, but a common bird fit only to live in the woods. You stole those feathers from us. Give them back, you thief!"

The other peacocks, angry at being tricked, started to peck the jay, and soon he had lost all the peacock feathers, as well as many of his own. The poor bird only just managed to escape with his life. After regaining his breath in the fig tree, he sadly limped home.

His mother and father did not scold him for being foolish. They fed him juicy worms while he recovered. When he got better, his father showed him how to hide acorns when they ripened. The jay had great fun learning to call out like other birds and imitating the sounds of cats and lambs—a marvelous talent that all jays are blessed with. He never envied those dreadful peacocks again, but he was quite happy just to be himself.

· MORAL ·
Fine feathers don't make a fine bird.

· THE END ·